CITY / COUNTRY

A Car Trip in Photographs by KEN ROBBINS

VIKING KESTREL

[1985]

To John Berg
for his friendship
and his faith in me.

VIKING KESTREL
Viking Penguin Inc., 40 West 23rd Street, New York, New York 10010, U.S.A.
Penguin Books Ltd, Harmondsworth, Middlesex, England
Penguin Books Australia Ltd, Ringwood, Victoria, Australia
Penguin Books Canada Limited, 2801 John Street, Markham, Ontario, Canada L3R 1B4
Penguin Books (N.Z.) Ltd, 182–190 Wairau Road, Auckland 10, New Zealand

First published in 1985 by Viking Penguin Inc.
Published simultaneously in Canada

Printed in Japan by Dai Nippon Printing Company Ltd.
Set in Galliard.
1   2   3   4   5   89   88   87   86   85

Library of Congress Cataloging-in-Publication Data
Robbins, Ken.   City/Country.
Summary: Photographs and simple text capture the universal images
of a car trip, as seen from a child's backseat perspective.
[1. Travel—Fiction]   I. Title.
PZ7.R5327Ci 1985   [E]   85-40165   ISBN 0-670-80743-5

I like to remember the trips
we took from our home in the city
when I was young. Sometimes we drove
to the suburbs. And sometimes we drove
all the way to the country.

Now, many years later, all those
trips have merged in my memory.
What I remember best are not the
destinations or the people we
visited on any particular trip,
but the sights that we saw along
the way—so strange to me then,
so familiar now. They remain in my
mind like dreams.

We leave our high-rise apartment

and ride through the streets of the city,

stopping for people who are walking to work.

We ride past all the shining new buildings in midtown

and the crumbling older ones down by the docks.

Then we get on a bridge

or drive through a tunnel,

looking at the city as we leave it behind.

We drive on for miles of stop-and-go traffic,

past tenements sitting right by the road,

past factories and smokestacks,

past storage tanks bigger than houses or schools,

and out past the airport,

beyond all the discount stores,

shopping malls, parking lots, thousands of cars,

and the neat little houses with neat little lawns.

We get on the highway

for miles and miles,

with the big tractor trailers that go roaring by.

Then we get off and ride on the little back roads.

We read all the words on the billboards and signs,

we count all the dairy cows,

and we point out the barns.

And by the time we've passed the town,

out beyond the country store,

the sun has set and we're glad to be...

up in the mountains

or down by the sea.